Vegan Love Jones

Jordan Young

DEDICATION

This book is dedicated to you. I appreciate everyone who bought this book, and I hope that you love it and recommend it to your friends.

CONTENTS

Jordan Young

ACKNOWLEDGMENTS

I give thanks to the Most High; without my gifts of writing and teaching I wouldn't be able to do what I love to do the most. Thank you, Most High, for your love, mercy, and consistency. You take good care of me, and I am very thankful. Please don't ever leave my side, and I promise to inform the world that you are my true source of power.

CHAPTER 1
IN THE CUSTODY OF MY PAST

It's been a long two months since my last noteworthy date. Actually, it's only been long in the physical since I've been thinking about Jenise every day since the night that we were together. Almost every day I replay many of our conversations both out loud and in my mind as a way of staying sane. It might be what's driving me insane now that I think about it, but that's neither here nor there.

My days have been running together over the last two months, and a part of me feels as if I've been missing out on life by replaying and being a prisoner of my past. I get a certain rush though when thinking about our time together. Thinking of her voice has been bringing me comfort in my time of grief. I can replay her laugh with ease in my mind, and I sometimes even pretend that we are in a room together having a conversation. But when I snap out of my delusional world of love and happiness, I hurt even more than I did before I started pretending.

It's crazy how it works. I start missing her, which leads to a feeling of loneliness and depression and so I start thinking of her, replaying all the moments with her that brought me joy. I even play out, in my mind, conversations and events that never took place, which bring euphoric feelings that are priceless for a person unable to find joy independently of such delusions. I clutch my pillow at night as if Jenise was lying next to me with the cold pillow case representing her body in need of my warm embrace.

When I stop pretending is when things start to hurt, but the high that I reach when fantasizing has helped me to rationalize my addictive, painful, and, to be frank, pitiful behavior. I've let two months pass me by without much effort into advancing my professional life or seeking a love life, something that I think we all need to feel complete. Don't get me wrong: I definitely think each person is responsible for finding inner peace and joy independently of another being, but without love, I say, life is sad and empty regardless of the amount of money or fame that a person has come to obtain.

It's not that I don't plan to move on, it's just that it isn't as easy as it would appear from listening to all the rap songs that talk about moving from one love to the next without hesitation or delay. I haven't listened to much country music in my lifetime, but I think, from the few songs that I have heard, country music artists are much more accurate when describing the dissolution process of a love interest.

Speaking from experience, there is nothing simple about walking away from love. Not when that love brought you uncontrollable laughs, sexy outbursts, and a soulful voice that could bring a raging lion to peace. We were only talking for a few weeks, but a countless number of times she would anger me and then change her tone and speak to me the way that only she could. My guard would instantly be abandoned. No defense was needed for a women obviously sent from the gods to bring joy on earth to any man who was lucky enough to be chosen by her. I was convinced that I had lived as a great, giving, selfless man in a past life and that she was my reward.

I say all that to say that I miss Jenise. I miss her a lot. I clearly haven't helped myself much with my addictive behavior over the last two months, but she was the only girl that made me feel the way that she made me feel. As cliché as it sounds, I thought she was the one. I was all but certain that I would never have to visit another club, bar, or bookstore in search of a compatible companion. True, companions are easy to find, but finding one on the same page with similar values seemed like a fairytale until I met Jenise.

Not only was she beautiful, which to me means pretty with a compassionate heart, but she also had class, confidence, and could wear a $25 outfit and look like a runway model. Her walk, which changed depending on her mood, was always sexy and enticing.

I had so many visions of her. Our relationship extended beyond reality. In my mind we went on more than just one date. In my mind we had several arguments. In my mind, even when she was angry, I loved watching her leave my apartment only to wish that she would get in and out of her car and return to my apartment. And occasionally she did, cursing me out before embracing me and demanding, with her body language, that we make passionate love. I loved fighting with her, and sometimes I even purposely started fights with her because she was so damn sexy when she was upset.

On top of her beauty and charm she was also a vegan, which meant the world to me. Her passion for animals was seductive. She believed that we as humans couldn't truly live in peace with one another as long as we were willing to support the torture and killing of innocent animals. She felt as if we should treat animals the way that we'd want to be treated if a superior being came to Earth that had the ability to physically control and exert their wills over us. I totally agreed with her.

I had already been vegan for a year before we met. After seeing a couple of slaughterhouse videos there was no way that I could continue to support the way that those animals were being treated. Seeing cows and pigs hung upside down and having their throats slashed, only to be left hanging to die slowly, made me sick to my stomach. My heart and soul screamed out against the sight of man's cruelty. I couldn't just turn my back like many of my friends had been able to do after viewing videos that I had shared with them. I knew that if the tables were turned that I would be screaming to the heavens for mercy. And since I believe in karma, there is no way that I would ever want to do that to another being as I knew that I would only being doing it to myself.

It's funny how the universe works. I realize not many people are really paying attention though. Whenever I hear someone complain about something that makes them uncomfortable, my first thought is to help them recognize the energy that they put into motion that manifested itself in such a disharmonious way. Many people hate the idea of going within to fix what appears to be external problems, and I understand how in the physical realm it appears illogical. However, after careful observation of the universe, it is clear that the things that bother us the most are often a reflection of the energies within us that are outside of alignment with universal law.

Jenise was born and raised in New York, New York and her parents were highly educated. They gave her a hard time about being vegan, I later found out, and she often vented to me about how she felt so different from her family although she loved them very much. Her parents thought that not eating animals was extreme and attracted unnecessary attention. Being migrants to the United States, her parents thought it was very important to not rock the boat in any way and to fit in as best as possible with society's norms.

I never really believed in fitting in. I always thought it was best to just be yourself, seek to evolve, and strive to be better each day than you were the previous day. When I was a kid I used to talk to the Most High all of the time. One day, I promised to do whatever work He had for me and it's a promise that I've never forgotten. It actually makes me wonder. Was my purpose decided after I agreed to submit to the Most High or was it written in the plans prior to me arriving in the world? Some things we can only speculate about and this is one of them.

I grew up in Irving, Texas. About five minutes from Dallas. My parents named me Jordan after Michael Jordan, the retired basketball legend. My dad thought Michael Jordan, along with Muhammad Ali, were the most inspirational people in the world. As I grew up and studied numerology, the spiritual essence of numbers, I realized that Michael Jordan was so inspirational, in part, because he has the master number 11 life path number. The master number 11 represents the inspirational leader and often is a spiritual messenger. Michael Jordan was also gifted with a heightened sense of intuition and inspired millions of children and adults alike.

CHAPTER 2
FIRST IMPRESSIONS

Living in Dallas, I met Jenise at a local bookstore. She was reading several books about the history of Kemet, the land of Black faces, which is now known as Egypt. One of the books was *The Ankh: African Origin of Electromagnetism.*

"That book looks interesting. What are you reading?" I asked as the book cover with an image of a cross-like symbol with a loop on top next to the Sphinx in Egypt had me genuinely interested.

She looked up, paused for about three seconds, while maintaining eye contact, licked her lips, smiled, and went back to reading.

"All right...I'll just sit right here and read until you find the words to express yourself," I said while smiling. "I'm Jordan... like Michael," I said maintaining my smile and extending my hand.

She started laughing while maintaining a glow in her eyes. "Is that what you say to girls?" she asked.

"Excuse me?" I asked as I retrieved my hand.

"Is that your best line or something?"

"My best line?"

"Yeah, Jordan like Michael? Jordan isn't a hard name to understand or remember. Did you really have to let me know that you have a name connection to Michael Jordan?" she said while still laughing slightly.

"All right. Check this out. Let's start over… You have an interesting looking book in your hands. Is that like Egyptian Christianity or something? I actually really want to know," I said.

"So you expect me to just let you off the hook for that weak line?" she asked seriously.

"For the record, I don't use lines. But I did get you to start talking, so I guess it wasn't too weak. But I'll let you get back to your Christian studies," I said to put her on notice that I was willing to walk away.

"First of all I'm not a Christian or any other religion. If you spent more time in the bookstore you'd recognize that this isn't a Christian cross on my book. It's an ankh, the symbol of life from Kemet, which is the name for Ancient Egypt. The ankh is considered a connector to the divine energy of the universe. But you probably don't read much do you? You probably watch TV all day. You look like you sleep good in the matrix," she said with a soft, short laugh at the end, obviously testing me.

Her testing me actually helped my confidence. I knew that she would only be testing me if she was interested and wanted to see what I was made of.

"Can I buy you a coffee?" I asked.

"Coffee? Coffee is very acidic, dear. You really don't read do you?" she said.

"Wow," I responded, although it felt good to be challenged.

"You can buy me a green tea though," she said.

"If you say one more thing about my reading habits you're going to be buying me tea," I said.

She laughed. "Oh, yeah?"

"Yep. What's your name by the way? I'm Jordan."

"Didn't you already tell me your name, Michael?"

"Yeah, I did, but you didn't tell me your name, so I'm giving you another chance," I said.

"I don't know. I like boys that read. Can you read?" she asked with a serious look on her face.

"Wow," I said as I held back laughter in an attempt to hold on to whatever masculine frame I had left.

"No, I'm serious. If you can't read I don't need you walking up to me saying my name in front of people," she said.

"So you read a lot, huh?" I asked.

"I try to. What about you?"

"Yeah, I try to as well."

"Have you read anything interesting lately?" she asked as if she were genuinely interested.

"Actually I just finished a really good book about numerology, the spiritual study of numbers."

"I heard about numerology, but I haven't studied it yet. So wait, I'm about to learn something from a guy who doesn't even read that much?" she asked with a flirtatious smile.

"I bet that's really unfortunate for you, huh?"

"It really does feel that way... I'm Jenise," she said extending her hand.

It was only her name, but I felt as if I was officially on first base. We walked to the other side of the bookstore to get some tea, but we didn't talk much. Something told me to just feel the energy that she was emitting, and I maintained my cool until she broke the silence.

"You like my energy, don't you?" she asked as we were about to arrive at the ordering counter.

"You haven't turned me off yet if that's what you're asking, but I don't know. I have to be around you some more before I know if I like it or not," I said not wanting to give her validation. I've learned from experience that many women get turned off if they win you over too easily, and I wanted her to know that she'd have to earn my time and attention day-by-day based on how she carried herself.

"Whatever, your eyes snitched you out a long time ago. You're probably planning our future already like most guys who lose their minds after one conversation with an attractive girl. Is that you?" she asked.

"Nah, I don't think that far ahead. Actually, I'm only focused on you buying this green tea, so I'm hoping you give me a reason to make you pay," I said.

"You know what? I should not expect a man who doesn't read to have any money. Unless you're a beggar. You have a sign?"

"I'm an Aquarius actually," I replied proudly.

"Not your astrology sign, stupid," she said while laughing. "I'm talking about those signs that people hold up asking for money," she said.

"Wow, you don't stop do you?" I said letting out a little bit of laugher.

"Actually, I don't," she said before ordering two green teas with added agave.

"I would say thank you, but then it wouldn't be punishment for your bad behavior," I said.

"Finally," She said.

"Finally what?"

"Finally a brother who thinks I should be punished for my bad behavior," she said as if she intentionally misbehaves all the time.

"So you like being punished, huh?" I asked seductively.

"Maybe," she replied.

"Why did you add agave to our teas?" I asked.

"It's an alkaline sweetener that I learned about from Dr. Sebi. You know Dr. Sebi?" she asked.

"Yeah, I've seen a few of his videos on YouTube. I haven't studied him much though," I replied.

"So agave is considered alkaline and it helps to reduce the level of acidity in your body. The more acidic your body, judged by pH levels, the more likely you are to get sick. So I try to stay away from acidic foods whenever possible, including coffee," she said.

"I see," I said as I took a sip from my tea while thinking of the next thing to say. I reminded myself to speak on an observation whenever I need something to keep the conversation going. "So your book about the ankh looks interesting. Can you tell me more about that?" I asked.

"Sure. Well basically, the ankh is the key to experiencing electromagnetism. Electromagnetism is when there is interaction between electric fields and magnetic fields. Our skin is highly electric because of our rich melanin levels. Our melanin acts as an organic semiconductor that works in conjunction with the ankh. The ankh is a high frequency oscillator, which means it produces electric currents by non-mechanical means. The ankh safely produces high voltages, which is one of the many reasons it looks like I'm glowing. I have my ankh necklace on under my shirt. They say the ankh can be used to power our homes and cars, but I can't attest to the validity of that personally. You should get one though. I felt its power immediately. I rarely ever take mine off. My sixth sense became just as capable of serving me as my other senses after I got my ankh. I actually knew you were going to approach me and ask me about my book as soon as I saw you. I predict lots of stuff nowadays, and I experience constant synchronicity," she said leaving me impressed.

"That was a lot. Were you a science major or something?" I asked.

"No, but I read this book a few times already and another one called *P.T.A.H. Technology: Engineering Applications of African Sciences*. I understood the books just well enough to know that I should keep my ankh close to me.

"Indeed. Sounds like some good stuff," I said while taking a seat at an empty table. "When's your birthday?" I asked.

"December 7th, why?" she asked.

"That explains it."

"Explains what?" she said insecurely.

"The seven is very spiritual in numerology. People with sevens in their numerology profiles often value spiritual wisdom, are intellectual, and are usually seekers of truth. Sounds like you?" I asked.

"Even if it didn't, who would admit that

they don't value spiritual wisdom and are stupid and okay with being manipulated?" she said while laughing.

"I guess you have a point. When is your full birthday?" I asked.

"Why, you're going to stalk me if I don't give you my number?" she asked.

"I haven't stalked anyone since college. You should be safe," I replied tongue-in-cheek.

"Fine. My birthday is December 7, 1993," she said.

"Okay, give me a second while I do the math," I said while doing the math mentally. "It looks like you're a life path 5, which means you need change, freedom, and travel is very important to you. You're also a bit of a risk taker it seems," I said. "I also imagine that you're socially confident."

"Wow, that sounds so accurate. How did you calculate that?" she asked.

"To figure out a life path number, the easiest thing to do is to enter your birthdate into Google and type the words 'life path number' next to your birthdate in the search bar. But to figure it without Google, you have to add up the reduced month that you were born, with the reduced day you were born, and then the reduced year you were born. For example, your month was December, which is 12. But with numerology, you add up the numbers until you get a single digit. So with 12, 1 + 2 = 3. December is represented by 3. The day you were born is 7, but if you were born on the 16th, that would be 7 too since 1 + 6 = 7. And for 1993, you add the 1 + 9 + 9 + 3 to get 22. The 22 reduces to 4. So then you add the 3 from December with the 7 and the 4 from 1993 for a total of 14, which is reduced to 5 as 1 + 4 = 5," I said.

"Interesting. So is this like astrology?" she asked.

"Yes and no. They're both metaphysical sciences and they usually confirm each other. The biggest difference is that astrology provides more details and has a lot to do with the energies that affect us from the heavens. Numerology deals with interpreting numbers and names," I said hoping to impress her as well but without looking like I was trying to impress her. I didn't want to come off as a try-hard.

"That's very interesting. You should write me a research paper on numerology so I can learn it without having to read a bunch of books," she said obviously testing me again for compliance.

"Okay, yeah, that's cool. You need me to

cut your grass and fold your laundry too," I said being sarcastic.

We started laughing simultaneously. "Let me buy you an alkaline drink sometime. Give me your number so I can repay you for the green tea," I said.

"I thought me buying the green tea was my punishment?"

"It was, but I plan on misbehaving too, and you'll probably need an energy drink when I'm done," I said slowly trying to plant the idea of sex into her mind.

"Put your number in my phone and call yourself so you can have my number," she said while handing me her phone and looking turned on.

I took the phone and entered my number. I decided not to call myself though to show her that I wasn't desperate for her phone number. I also wanted her to know that I was confident that she'd want to talk to me again.

"Well I should run now. It was nice meeting you and talking to you. And thanks for the numerology info," she said while reaching one arm out for a hug.

I hugged her back with both arms and let go after about three or four seconds. I liked her a lot, and I wanted her to get used to me being physical with her. She needed to know that our relationship would be mental, spiritual, and physical.

CHAPTER 3
IT'S A VIBE

It was about two weeks since I put my number into Jenise's phone at the bookstore and I hadn't heard from her. Although I never lost confidence in myself, I was beginning to lose confidence in my chances of building with her. It was about 7:30 PM on a Friday evening when my phone started vibrating. I thought that it was my friend Chris since we had just finished texting about a party that he wanted me to attend that Saturday night with some of our friends.

"I think you forgot something at the bookstore," the text read.

I immediately got excited when I saw the text and I knew exactly who it was. I started to respond right away, but didn't want to give the impression that I was desperate or lonely, so I decided to wait until the next morning to respond. The last thing I wanted to do was to make her think that I had no plans on a Friday night.

"Hey, I was hanging with friends last night. How are you?" I replied the next morning around 10:00 AM.

"I'm good. How r u?"

"I'm good. No complaints. What did I leave at the bookstore?" I said assuming that she was talking about me not calling myself with her phone so that I would have her number.

"Obviously your mind. Did I hurt your feelings, poor thing?"

"How did you hurt my feelings? Did I give you the impression that I hurt easily or something?"

"Kind of. You were obviously into me, so I figured something made you change your mind about taking me out."

"I actually tried to call you a few days after we met and then I realized that I didn't have your number," I replied.

"Oh… I thought you called yourself with my phone," her reply read.

"I thought I did too, but it must didn't go through. Are you available next Saturday?"

"I'm not sure yet, but I'm available tonight. You have plans for tonight already?"

Her text put me into a tough spot. Once again I didn't want her to think that I didn't have a life. At the same time, however, I really wanted to see her. I went back and forth mentally for about 20 minutes before I replied.

"I promised a couple of my friends that I'd attend a party later tonight."

"That sucks. I was hoping to hear more about my numerology profile."

"Let's do next Saturday. I'll even let you order a refill to reward you for your patience," I said.

"That's so generous of you."

"Cool?"

"That works!"

"Okay, I'll call you next Saturday. You can give me your address when I call."

"Only because you said you haven't stalked anyone since college. I usually don't let people know where I live."

"Wow, you remember that?"

"Yep, see you Saturday," she said ending our dialogue.

After ending our conversation, I was excited and decided to use my abundance of energy to go to the gym. I decided against going to the party that my friend Chris was pressuring me to attend. I just wasn't in the mood to be around a lot of new people. Being an Aquarius, I was naturally in the mood to daydream. When I got back home I showered and started planning for the following weekend.

The week leading up to our date seemed to vanish and I noticed that the thought of seeing her again made my hands sweat. I didn't usually get nervous before a date, but I wasn't clueless to the fact that I was digging her like not many other girls that I've dated.

About 4:00 PM on the day of our date I called her to confirm and to let her know what time I would come over to pick her up.

"Hello," she said in her most feminine voice as she answered the phone.

"Hey…," I responded wanting to take the conversation slowly.

"Hey…," she responded matching my vibe.

"I was wondering if 7:00 works for you tonight."

"Yeah, 7:00 is cool. You want my address now?"

"Can you text it to me?"

"Yeah, that's fine. Can you text me when you're on your way though?"

"Yes, that's cool. I have to finish some work on a project that I'm working on, but I'll text you around 6:30. Unless, of course, I find out after you text me your address that you're my next-door neighbor or something."

"Okay, Mr. Funny. I'll text you my address right now," she said once again ending the dialogue.

I arrived at her house around 6:55. She came out about two minutes later.

"Nice to see you," she said as she got into my car.

"Likewise."

"So where are we going?"

"I thought we'd try something different… It's a surprise though. So close your eyes and just feel the drive," I said, subconsciously trying to put her mind on sex once again.

"How do I know I'm safe if I close my eyes?"

"Look at me…," I said while staring intently into her eyes hoping to further develop our connection.

She looked into my eyes and it felt like there was a volcano inside of me getting ready to erupt. "Oh shit" I thought to myself. I don't know how she did it but when we locked eyes it felt as if our souls immediately merged. My only concern was turning her off by showing too much interest.

"Boy, what are you thinking?" she asked

sweetly.

"About how safe you are with me."

"Is that all you're thinking?"

"I don't think and tell," I said as I pulled into the street and smashed the gas. I wanted her to feel me without me touching her and I think I accomplished my goal.

"Boy, shit!"

"You're all right. Just try to relax. You're in good hands with me. I promise," I said locking eyes once again.

After driving for about three minutes, I decided to try my luck and I placed my hand on the top of her thigh. She immediately slapped my hand, but she locked eyes again and this time the passion was clearly becoming more intense within the both of us.

"Just trying to feel your heartbeat," I said seductively.

"Pull over," she said in a tone that didn't reveal much information.

"Right here?" I asked pointing.

As soon as I pulled over she put her hand behind my head and pulled me in for what was the most passionate kiss that I had ever had in my entire life.

"I don't usually kiss on the...," I said before she pulled me closer and attacked my mouth again with hers.

We were parked not far from a busy street, but I was prepared to have sex with her right there in the car. I didn't care if we got caught. I was worked up and didn't want to stop. But after kissing for about five minutes, she let me go.

"Can you take me home?"

"Excuse me?" I said confused. I didn't know if she wanted to end the date or if she wanted to go somewhere more private.

"My place or yours?"

"Do you really need to ask?" she said in a lustful voice while locking eyes.

I immediately turned around and headed back to my place. We were there in less than 10 minutes it seemed. We didn't talk while I was driving back to my place, but when I put my hand back on her thigh she put her hand on top of mine. At that moment I knew it was on. "It's a vibe" is what I thought to myself and I hurried home.

CHAPTER 4
12 HOURS

We made love from around 7:45 PM until early morning the next day. While making love, we kissed passionately, stared into each other's eyes, and seemed to not be able to get enough of each other. It helped that we played Jacquees' song "Wow" on repeat throughout much of the night. I played the song for her in the car on the way back to my place and when we got to my place she made sure to request it again.

I had been vegan for over a year and it showed. I had what appeared to be limitless stamina and desire to be one with her mind, body, and soul. She, on the other hand, moved her body like she had found the lover that she had been praying for ever since her first heartbreak. In addition to being loud with everything, including her moans, she scratched my back and my chest, drawing a little blood from both.

It was an amazing night and, even though it lasted until the next morning, time seemed to move too fast for my liking. We had somehow built up a great amount of tension, and I was determined not to end the love making until all of the tension had dissipated.

"I think I should go now," she said around 7:00 in the morning after gently sucking my bottom lip.

"Where else would you rather be?" I said as I turned up the intensity of my stroke, which unleased an ocean of emotion within her.

"I really have to go," she said as she pushed me to my back and put herself on top and started a very intense grind looking down into my eyes.

Although I've had women into me like this in the past, Jenise had me thinking about making her my girlfriend and connecting like this every night if I could. I didn't want to reveal what I was thinking about, but I knew that she was extremely insightful and she had already pointed out to me that my eyes were not loyal when it came time to keep the secrets of my heart.

"It's too soon to fall in love," she said

with a cocky smile after we locked eyes as we finished making love.

"You're your own support system, huh? Tell yourself whatever you need to keep yourself sane," I said with a slight smile, pretending that she didn't just read my mind perfectly.

"You saying I wasn't good?" she asked sounding concerned.

"Wow, I didn't think you were the type that needed confirmation."

"I don't need confirmation. I just wanted to see what you sound like when you're telling a lie."

"What you need that intel for? You're not making future plans already are you? I think I want to play hard to get now. Tell me why I shouldn't?" I asked without a hint of seriousness in my voice and body language.

"You can't play hard to get if I know I already have you. Your mother never taught you to be a challenge?" she said softly, but I couldn't tell if she was serious or not.

"I'm thinking if I give you a serious answer you're probably going to say that I failed some silly test or something," I said laughing.

"You know what? I do test men a lot. But you know what else? You guys need to be tested," she said sounding as if she believed her own words.

"You think we need to be tested? What do you think that says about you if you feel the need to constantly test men? And how has that been working for you? I bet the guys that pass your tests are really honorable aren't they?" I said revealing a slight amount of irritation to the practice of constant female testing.

"So what are you saying?"

"What do you mean? I meant what I said. I'm surprised you haven't read any books revealing the secrets to harmony. Tests are not the way. Tests only cause disharmony, which the universe must return to you. A lot of times this disharmony is returned on the mental plane only, and then the woman wonders why her self-esteem is low or why she can't maintain happiness. A woman, or a man for that matter, should be able to go within when deciding if a person is a worthy partner. In my opinion, a woman repeatedly testing a man shows a lack of trust in her own intuition. And women have been using the same types of tests for decades. No offense, but it's not a coincidence that the men that pass those ridiculous tests most often are usually not honest or self-respecting guys themselves," I said, hoping I didn't come off as lecturing.

"You sound like you've been giving this some thought."

"I think most men have actually. You don't trust yourself or something?" I asked actually wanting to know.

"I do, but it's just something that I've always done. And men don't usually talk to me like this... I can get what you're saying though for sure. I never thought about how my tests caused disharmony. I definitely believe in karma, but for some reason I've never made the connection. I've done a lot of crazy stuff just to see how my guy responds."

"The way I look at it, everything is connected. The whole universe. Your thoughts right here in this room are affecting the vibrations of the whole universe," I said.

"I agree with that. That's one of the reasons why I went vegan," she said bringing joy to my ears.

"I didn't know you were vegan. How long? I asked trying not to sound too excited.

"Almost four years. Since my last year in college. Have you ever considered it?"

"Yeah, I've been vegan for over a year now. You couldn't tell by my endurance?" I said with glowing eyes and confidence.

"Boy, be quiet. You are so nasty. For real though... Are you really vegan?"

"Yeah, I saw some slaughterhouse videos that really messed me up. I had no idea the animals were treated so badly."

"It's so horrible! That's what got me too. I saw them smashing a baby piglet's head on the ground, and then they put all the boy chickens in a grinder alive and I started crying. I saw how the female cow cries after they take her baby away. I had no idea that the animals felt so much pain, both emotionally and physically. They literally are in the slaughterhouses screaming for mercy," she said revealing her compassionate nature.

"Finally a woman more compassionate than me" I thought to myself. This was a major turn on, but I didn't want to show too much interest. She already mentioned the word challenge and so I had to keep my cool regardless of how perfect I was starting to think that she was for me.

"Don't' let this go to your head, but I don't usually meet a lot of guys like you... Most guys stop vibing with me once I start talking about the stuff that I really care about. Like, they usually look down on veganism, and most of them can't hold conversations about anything other than sex, cars, or football. It's always refreshing to click with someone with similar interests as yourself. Maybe you should start playing hard to get," she said with a wink.

"What you don't realize is that I am hard to get. I don't have to play like anything. You think any woman can hold my interest? I need to be turned on by the mental and the physical before I even want to exchange numbers with a female. And after we exchange numbers she has to qualify spiritually and emotionally. I like a woman with fortitude and some sense of how the universe works. See, you just barely made the cut," I said smiling, turning our serious conversation playful once again, causing her to smile and lock eyes with me.

"I barely made the cut? Whatever. Can I use your shower?" she said in a playful mood as she left the bed and headed toward the bathroom.

"Sure, there are some towels in there that you can use."

After occupying the bathroom for about 30 minutes, she came out in a towel. She stood still seductively for about a second, locked eyes, and rushed me again. We started kissing and I couldn't wait to become one with her again.

"Last round... make sure you get enough,"

she said as we were going at it passionately again. We made love for another 45 minutes, and I enjoyed every second. I believe in always doing my best with whatever I'm doing, and I lived up to my own standard with the way I was in sync with her the whole time physically, spiritually, mentally, and emotionally. It was an amazing connection.

We finished making love around 9:00 AM, and she kissed me on my cheek before leaving. I tried to kiss her on the lips but she turned her head weirdly and gave me her cheek. I offered to take her home, but she said that she had already called for an Uber since she needed to have her driver make a couple of stops on her way home. After the way we had just connected sexually and spiritually, I wasn't too worried about the way she exited. I figured it was probably just another test that she didn't even know that she was doing.

About four days after we hooked up, I called her around 7:00 PM on a Wednesday night to ask her out. I didn't get an answer, so I left a voice message asking if she wanted to meet at my favorite vegan restaurant in the city the following Saturday night. Based on our connection, I expected her to call me back right away. However, the day ended without a text or a return call. In fact, the week ended the same way. No call or text. I was tempted to call her again, but I knew that women who like to test men a lot usually consider it a failed test if he calls or texts her twice before allowing her a chance to respond.

Soon, it was a whole month without hearing from her. Then it was two. I didn't understand where I went wrong. Did I show too much interest? Was the sexual connection not as strong as I thought it was? Was it possibly too strong? Did she have a boyfriend? I didn't know what to think and for two months I thought about everything.

I became obsessive with my thoughts. They were all about her and I didn't like it. She was right. I was planning the future from the beginning and now I'm left to wonder if that's why she ghosted me. One thing my mom did teach me is that no woman wants a man who's too eager to be with a woman. Women like men with options. My mother used to always tell me that most women like to battle other women to win the affection of a man that they perceive to be of high value. I didn't think I was easy, but I guess I wasn't difficult either.

It was now Saturday evening, about two months after my night with Jenise when I heard a knock on the door.

"Who is it?" I yelled.

Nobody responded and so I went to the door. When I looked through the peep hole I was excited to see her beautiful face, and her hair was done perfectly. It was long and straight. She obviously remembered me mentioning that I was a sucker for straight hair. My heart started beating quickly. My hands started sweating. Her makeup, dress, and body language were all grabbing my attention as I looked through the peep hole. I opened the door slowly. We locked eyes without speaking for about five long seconds. I was waiting for her to explain herself, and I think she was waiting for me to make it easy on her.

"Are you going to invite me in?"

I had to be quick on my feet. I wasn't sure what to do. I didn't want her to view me as easy to win over, but I also didn't want to ruin my chance to become one with who I had been thinking was the perfect girl. If such a thing even existed. I had a strong feeling that this was a test of some sort. I had been through a lot during the two months since I was last with her and I knew that I would have to make her pay for her bad behavior. She wouldn't respect me if I didn't.

Jordan Young

CHAPTER 5
NEXT IMPRESSIONS

"To be honest, I didn't appreciate how you disappeared for the last couple of months. And now you think you can just show up here like everything is cool?" I said calmly.

"Well I had to see if I could trust myself. You asked me if I trusted myself. I told you that I could but then I needed to prove it to myself. You know what I mean?" she said as if she wanted me to be understanding and gentle.

"And what do you mean by that? You should probably say a little more if you expect to get inside my place," I said, accidently revealing to her that I really wanted a reason to let her in my apartment.

"Look, the truth is I've relied on testing men that I'm interested in as a way to see who's the best fit for me, and you were right.

The results have been not so good for me so far," she said and then paused, possibly looking for weakness.

There was certainly weakness within me that wanted to just snatch her up, make love to her for 24 hours straight, and talk about everything else later. But I knew that if I took that route that she would likely have difficulty respecting me if I made it so easy on her.

"So what are you saying?" I asked.

"I wanted to see if I could truly trust myself… My intuition told me that you would call me that following Wednesday or Thursday to ask me out… And I was right. I also knew that if I didn't answer the phone that you would leave me a voice message. And I was right again. I was also willing to bet money that despite how much you were feeling me that you had enough self-respect that if I didn't call you back that you wouldn't harass me and keep calling me. I was right again…. It may have been a test, but I was only testing myself this time."

"So what did you get from all of this?"

"I proved to myself that I can trust myself. And that you're worthy of me putting my trust in you as well…If that's something that you want still."

"Look, two months is a long time… You're

going to have to make it up to me in a major way… I have a couple of things in mind, but you're going to have to figure out some additional ways to make things up to me; otherwise, I'm not interested," I said impressing myself.

"I was hoping you would say something like that... Let me show you something real quick," she said seductively as she gently placed her hand on my chest and walked past me and into my apartment.

I immediately grabbed her arm as she walked past me and I aggressively pulled her close to me. She appeared to be caught off guard for a brief moment before I started kissing on her neck and pulling up her dress. She matched my passion and intensity until the next morning. Once again, time moved too quickly for me and the night was even more electric than our first night together. I was totally conscious of the fact that I might not ever see her again and if that was the case I wanted to give her everything that I had to give physically, mentally, emotionally, and, most importantly, spiritually. I knew that if I cherished every moment that I could live with the outcome if she happened to disappear again. But I've always known that many women correlate good sex to love, and the way I gave it to her throughout the night, I was confident that she would view me as the demi-god that I am.

"How am I supposed to play fair with you if you're going to be making love to me like that? It's not fair what you're doing to me," she said as if she was a victim of some sort from under the covers.

"I thought we did it to each other," I said seductively with a smile as I rose out of bed. "And plus, who knows when you'll be back. I had to make it count. Give you something to think about."

"All I want to think about is how safe I feel with you. You make me feel so comfortable, Jordan. That's no lie. I feel like I'm connected to the power of the Creator when I'm with you and I've never felt that before," she said locking eyes with a sincere looking glow.

Her words touched me in a way that was quite unfamiliar. Was she simply telling me the things that she knew that I believed about myself or was she genuinely expressing herself and simply reflecting back to me the energy that I had been putting into the universe ever since I had become acquainted with my divine nature?

I went to the shower hoping for company but she never joined. When I got out the shower I found her in a deep sleep, snoring in my bed. She looked comfortable, which made me happy. Even though I was convinced that she had good intentions this time around, I knew that I was in trouble concerning my feelings for her, but I didn't really care. Because of how I felt when I was with her, it was worth the risks. All the risks. She was pure inspiration if I had ever known it. The match that sparks desire and creation. I had the will to accomplish anything after being in her presence. A part of me even wanted to believe that the Most High created her as my secret weapon. That's how I felt when we were near each other.

I decided to meditate and then get some work done on a design that I had been creating while she was sleeping. It was a special art piece that was going to be displayed at an art show downtown. She slept until about two in the afternoon.

"What are you drawing?" she asked after finding her way into my art room.

"I haven't given it a name yet, but when I have emotions that I can't describe with words, I work on this piece right here."

"It's beautiful... In some type of way I can hear what it's saying, but I can't describe it with words... What are you going to call it?"

"I don't' know yet. I've been through a few names so far. I've considered naming it Undiscovered Words or Words with Energy. You like either of those?"

"Yeah, those are both good names for it. Where do you keep all of your artwork, Jordan?" she asked with excitement.

"I try to keep everything on display somewhere. I have a couple pieces at vegan restaurants and a few more at art museums, mostly here in Dallas."

"I never even asked what you do. Is this your thing?"

"I do love to draw. It's actually pretty therapeutic. I sometimes have feelings that are indescribable and this is the best way for me to have an outlet. But I work as a financial advisor. I help people manage their money. Most people don't understand the power of compounding and I make believers out of everyday people and have already placed thousands on the road to financial freedom. I really like my work," I said proudly with a smile.

"Wow, look at you. Vegan and financially literate. You do any work with private equities or just public?"

"Did she just ask me an investment question?" I thought to myself. "What do you know about investing?" I asked.

"I actually run a small venture capital fund."

"Are you serious?" I asked with a little too much excitement.

"Yes and no. It's my family's money mostly. My dad has a lot of money connections back in New York, and I ended up interning for a VC fund in college. I managed my own money for a couple of years after college, and for the last few years I've been managing my family's money in a fund that mixes public and private investments. It's been really fun."

"How long have you been interested in investments?" I asked.

"Since high school. I read *Rich Dad Poor Dad* and have been thinking about how to make my money work for me ever since. But my favorite is definitely *Generational Wealth: Beginner's Business & Investing Guide*. I totally get the concept of treating my money as an employee whose job it is to earn more money for me while I do all of the things that I enjoy. It clicked with me right away. What about you?"

"Probably since my first year of college. I read *Rich Dad Poor Dad* too, but before that I read *One Up on Wall Street* by Peter Lynch and

I've been interested ever since. I read *Generational Wealth* also. It's definitely one of my favorites. And I didn't just want to get wealthy for myself. I wanted to educate as many people as possible. A lot of my clients get really excited when I show them how a one-time $5,000 investment at 14% annual growth over 30 years can turn into a small, tax-free fortune when done in a Roth IRA."

"What does the math turn out to on $5k over 30 years at 14%, smart guy?" she asked.

"About $250,000. And I put most of my clients in the technology sector exchange traded fund XLK, and I also make sure that they sign up for dividend reinvestment. They are usually surprised at the long-term difference in growth when the dividends are automatically reinvested."

"That is such a turn on," she said smiling with her hip poking out. "An artist that's also into finance. So, yeah, we definitely can't be together now. Because I know you are going to want to manage our money and I've already made plans for your salary," she said with her glowing smile. "Let me guess, you write poetry too?"

"Actually, when I'm inspired, I can put together a really nice piece. I'm usually pretty good at putting my feelings into words. But this piece right here is just for when I can't."

"Have you been inspired to write any poetry lately?"

"Yeah, I have, actually. Why, you want to hear something?"

"Yeah, for sure. What do you have?"

"Alright, this one is one of my recent favorites. I haven't given it a name yet, though…If my Father, the Most High, approves…there are some things by way of demonstration that I would like, no pardon me for being polite, that I need to share with you. It's physical, metaphysical, and sexual. And just when you thought a man couldn't possibly dig any deeper, I'll introduce you to the spiritual. So go ahead and send your energy my way. My plan is to take you to a higher space and turn our love session into a lifelong vacay…Do you need to breathe, baby? Pardon me for the silly questions…Cause a man's job is to listen to what your body and spiritual vibration has to say. 'Go deeper, go deeper, go deeper,' and a silent 'yes ma'am' is how I reply. How I respond to this incredible bond. If it's as good as it is in my dreams, we'll need a thousand pillows to drown out your impeccable screams. I can do you right. I mean, I can go all night… It's so many benefits to being a vegan, girl, so tell me… is you bout that life? You are what you eat, so I'll be you in a minute. Rounds 2, 3, 400, ain't no limit when I'm up in it. Before I touch your body say my grace before I taste it. Your love is so pure I would never ever waste it. Give you all that you need you'll never have to fake it. I know you feel this vibration, we're a match let's just face it… When you look me in the eye I go from patient to impatient and waiting. I'm ready when you are. Heard of chance? Let's just take it…" I shared smoothly and confidently, making eye contact as I finished.

"Oh my god, Jordan. Did you really write that?"

"Yeah, I found some inspiration a while back. It's one of many."

"That was really dope. And all facts. Wow, you are really incredible, Jordan."

"Thank you… It's really cool that you see me in the same light that I see myself," I said with a smile.

"Okay, you're getting big headed now," she said with a laugh.

"No, but thank you, I appreciate your words," I said a little more seriously.

"You ever have sex in here?" she asked hinting that she wanted to use my creative space for more than just creating artwork.

"Mostly just in my mind..." I said as I turned to face her. "You've done some pretty generous things for me in this room," I said seductively as I lifted her head back using my finger under her chin. I kissed her gently for about two seconds before we both turned up the intensity. We used every wall in the room as a prop. Having a deep intimate connection with her, I enjoyed our intimacy the most when I was standing and her legs were wrapped around my waste. I could see and feel all of her love in that position. While standing in her embrace I felt unstoppable. I felt protected and exalted by the divine energy that permeates the universe. This was it!

CHAPTER 6
INSPIRATION

Jenise and I spent almost every day together for a few months after she came back. When we weren't working or spending time with family and close friends we were usually together. She spent a lot time at my place, but we spent a good amount of time together at her place as well. She had a lot of crystals at her house and the smells were always pleasant. She was everything that I had ever wanted in a woman. She was incredible, and her energy was my secret weapon.

I had drawn some of my best artwork, written some of my best poetry, and I even wrote a few great books with exceptional speed while engulfed in the fire of her inspiration. I've learned that inspiration is worth more than silver and gold, and that both nations and great fortunes have been built by the power of inspiration. Although our feelings for each other were well understood, we never directly verbally confessed our love to each other. I refused to say "I love you" first and I think she, being the natural tester that she was, wanted to see how long I could refrain.

However, we communicated non-verbally in the most intimate of ways. From our soul-sharing eye contact to our synchronistic movements, we were operating on the plane of love. Being spiritually conscious, I tried my best to take really good care of my karma as I didn't want the experience to fade before receiving all of the blessings for me that were stored within her.

I've learned from experience that mastering your energy and protecting your karma to the best of your ability makes it much easier to remain in harmony regardless of what challenges are encountered. Suffering is usually, if not always, more intense for the careless and unconcerned. I knew that the way that I carried myself in every other situation in life would have an effect on the reality that I created with Jenise. For at least three months, I was more attentive to my vibration than I had been in a really long time. I tried my best to not intentionally cause any disharmony.

The love that I felt and the inspiration that I received from her were great incentives for me to create consciously.

My intuition informed me that I didn't have to play any games with her and that she was mine for as long as it was in the best interest of the universe as a whole. I learned to trust my intuition, and so I made certain to make sure our relationship was a great benefit to the whole. She motivated me to do my Father's work even more than I was already driven. I knew that I was here to gain enlightenment and then to share it with the world. Before I met Jenise, I thought that achieving world peace, which is a common goal for an Aquarius, would be a multi-decade journey. However, once in her presence and one with her, I felt my power enhanced and I knew that I now had access to the divine power within me that was enough to do my Father's work.

Being an Aquarius, I was really turned on by her intellectual capacity. Her range was off the charts. She was so philosophical and often passionate concerning everything, including her intellectual pursuits. We talked about so many deep topics and explored the depths of each other mentally, emotionally, spiritually, and of course physically. In addition to my art room, the kitchen and bathroom counters were also used frequently to act out our mutual craving to be one with the other.

I often wondered what it meant when both the man and the woman felt connected to what seemed like the most powerful energy in the universe. I sincerely believed that my favor increased exponentially and that I had direct access to the power of the Most High when I was with her. And she had stated the same to me on several occasions, and being the believer in myself that I am, I believed her 100%. I was her god and she was my goddess. I knew that she was being honest with me because I was being honest with her. I had formed the habit early in childhood of being honest with everyone, unless, of course, I thought that the truth would cause some unnecessary embarrassment or some other form of unnecessary pain and suffering.

Although my feelings for her were not always able to be accurately and completely described with words, it is worth noting that a deep soul connection was clear. Whenever I would have an epiphany in her presence, she would instantly look to me to uncover my discovery. I could walk behind her slowly and gently and she would always know that I was there. Sharing extrasensory perception with another being is magnetic, addicting, and mentally fulfilling.

One of our most satisfying activities together was taking long walks and allowing our intuitions to guide us to those in need. Many people just needed a kind word or two, while others needed advice concerning the utilization of universal law to manifest their desired reality. When compelled, we'd choose random families for which we'd feed or buy groceries. One of the best parts of buying groceries for those in need was the opportunity that it created to speak to them while shopping about veganism, animal cruelty, karma, health, spirituality, and the importance of finding their purpose and pursuing the guided path.

Although I'm an Aquarius, my Venus is in Pisces. Your Venus sign represents your love nature and how you deal with relationships. I visited cafeastrology.com once I got acquainted with the metaphysical sciences and I was able to see in which zodiac signs my planets were located for a detailed analysis of which energies influence me, although I remain the master of the my fate.

I've always wanted to help the underdog and contribute, whenever possible, to them overcoming. I actually feel like in our current state that the entire world is in the underdog position as it would appear from the objective eye that the world is on a path of self-destruction. Although I wrote books and gave speeches in order to have an impact on more than one person at a time, there was something extraordinarily special about looking into someone's eyes after filling them with hope and inspiration. One of my greatest attributes from being an Aquarius is my humanitarian nature, and the best part of having my Venus in Pisces is my capacity to love unconditionally.

Growing up, I thought that only the Most High could love someone unconditionally, so I feel that by sharing this trait that I was at least partially created in my Father's image. Before I evolved to realize that true spirituality transcended all religion, I always admired the story of King David and the fact that he was considered a man of God's own heart. Being slightly jealous of King David's rumored relationship with the Most High, I would always pray for the Most High to make my heart like His own so that I would be a man of God's own heart as well.

As I got older, studied the metaphysical sciences, and gained knowledge of self, I realized that I was gifted with similar attributes as the rumored former King of Israel. Actually, I believe that we all have a unique set of gifts and if we were to focus our attention on them, we would all be in a constant state of gratitude, which would be demonstrated by perpetual praise and celebration.

I stayed aware of my power to co-create my own reality and I worked consciously to create the life that I wanted with Jenise. I didn't want to take things too fast, but, at the same time, I had a hard time taking breaks from spending time with her. Occasionally, my intuition would make it clear that I was becoming unbalanced by overindulging in our love and I'd reluctantly listen and take a day or two away from her to clean or meditate. I knew that staying balanced was a universal law and I didn't want my love to become a transgression. I worked hard to stay in alignment and everything in my life was going perfectly.

I was able to grow my client base as a financial advisor much quicker with Jenise than I had been able to without her. More importantly, I had been able to help convert hundreds of people to veganism during the months that we were together. Everything was perfect and I knew how to keep it that way. As I said, I knew that the keys to keeping my world intact were to stay mindful, take really good care of my karma, do my best in every area of life, and by making sure that all of my relationships and business projects were in the best interest of the whole. It's funny how when you really want something you become possessed by a force that drives you to obtain your target. I knew that my relationship with Jenise was as much of a relationship between me and the universe as it was a relationship between Jenise and I.

I officially knew what friends were talking about when they spoke of how their love interests keep them out of trouble. I always thought that they were referring to the damaging habit of picking sexual partners without proper discernment when single. However, from my own understanding, your woman keeping you out of trouble actually refers to her love and affection being used as a carrot by the universe to keep you in alignment. Even if this wasn't universal law, I was convinced that it was the law for me.

CHAPTER 7
MERCURY RETROGRADE

Three or four times a year the planet Mercury goes retrograde for about three weeks and appears, although not really, to move in reverse. Mercury rules communication and transportation, and it requires a lot more effort to succeed in these areas when Mercury is in retrograde. Many people hate when Mercury goes into retrograde because they often experience car problems, travel delays, broken cell phones, computer outages, misunderstandings, and more.

I've learned that Mercury retrograde is a great time to reflect, review, re-consider, re-plan, re-visit, re-calculate, and upgrade any work or projects that were "completed" prior to the retrograde. I've also learned that Mercury retrograde acts as a report card of sorts and the disharmony that we experience during a Mercury retrograde often is a reflection of our intentions and efforts during the preceding non-retrograde period.

Although we eventually studied astrology and numerology together, I shared with her the importance of communicating thoughtfully during the retrograde and how to have a relatively harmonious period. We established a complete list of guidelines to help us navigate the retrograde period. We agreed to not break up, sign any contracts, or buy any new cars or electronics during the retrograde. However, after four months of non-stop seeing each other, there was one very important subject that we never discussed and it just had to come up during the retrograde.

"Jordan…"

"What's up," I replied as I turned to face her while we were sitting on my couch.

"I think we need to talk."

"What's on your mind? Talk to me."

"What is this?"

"Excuse me?" I said implying that I needed clarification.

"Me and you… I know we have fun. I know we have this crazy connection. But where is this going?"

"I heard everything you said, but I'm not sure if I understand your question exactly."

"Are you my man? Are we together officially? Are you still seeing other girls? Because if you are I'm at the point where it has to stop. I'm too close to this situation for it to be undefined for much longer. Do you understand that?"

"You don't want to share my love and I dig that... I haven't even had the desire to be with another girl since we've been seeing each other. I'm actually the type of guy that doesn't need a commitment with someone in order to commit to that person. Do you catch what I'm saying?"

"It sounds like you telling me to not ask for a commitment because you're already committed... Is that what you're trying to say?"

"I'm not trying to say anything. I've been committed to the idea of building with you ever since the book store. But I also know that you need freedom and change."

"Wait, are you suggesting that I can't be in a committed relationship because I like freedom and change? Who in the hell doesn't like freedom and change?" she said as she got animated.

"No. What I'm saying is that I have no

desire to make you feel like your freedom is being taken away from you. I'm happy with things the way they are. I'm satisfied with what you bring to my life and I believe that you appreciate the value that I bring."

"So yes or no, man?"

"Whoa," I said as I was taken aback by her aggressiveness. "First of all, you're talking to me like I'm trying to play you or something. We've never discussed being in an exclusive relationship and the first time that you bring it up you think it's wise to deliver it with an ultimatum?"

"I didn't give you an ultimatum. I just don't want to be strung along."

"What? You can't be serious."

"No, you can't be serious! Up here acting like we married and you don't even claim me. You got me cleaning your house and cooking for you like I'm your wife, but all my clothes are still at my place like I'm still single. I don't like the deal that you're offering me anymore."

"Alright, let's calm down a little bit. I don't know what has gotten into you, but you are really in your fire element right now and I'm very tempted to blow some cool air your way," I said referring to my habit of gently blowing air at her on occasion when she got too fiery.

"Why are you playing with me? I asked you a serious question and I still haven't gotten a serious answer back yet. Dude, please, do not disrespect me. I'm starting to feel really disrespected right now."

"Can you please keep your cool. I promise I am not trying to play you or disrespect you in any kind of way, but the way you're approaching me isn't the way to get what you want," I said as I was starting to lose my patience with her.

"You know what, I don't really give a shit! I don't even know why I asked. Forget I said anything. I'll just keep letting you screw my head up while I wait for you to decide what you're going to do with me."

"What?"

"Exactly! It sounds so stupid! Quit trying to play me! You know what? Before I get angry I'm just going to just leave and I might not come back. You can let your other girls deal with this mess."

"I already told you that I wasn't seeing any other women. But I could if I wanted to because I'm a grown ass man who's not in a committed relationship with anyone. I'm not seeing anyone else because I don't want to see anyone else. Do you not understand that?" I said firmly but without losing my cool.

"You're still not even answering my question. I don't have time for this. I can't blame nobody but me. I can't believe I let you play me like this," she said with tears in her eyes as she headed for my door."

"Let me know when you're ready to finish this conversation like adults."

"There's nothing to talk about!" she yelled back in my direction after leaving my apartment and walking down a flight of stairs.

"Oh my god. What in the world got into this girl?" I thought to myself, forgetting that we were smack dead in the middle of Mercury retrograde. I was now left to wonder how in the world did I manifest this state of disharmony. I was a little confused because I tried my best to be good to Jenise and to everyone else in the world as well.

After much meditation and careful consideration, I came to the conclusion that the universe was providing the opportunity for me to reflect on my situation with Jenise and to provide more clarity of my intentions with her. In many ways she was right. I made love to her and connected with her with the intention of helping her develop a deep state of unconditional love and undying desire for me. After putting that type of energy into the universe, I now had a duty to close the deal and to make her feel more secure with our relationship. To do otherwise would have certainly been a transgression.

CHAPTER 8
LET'S BE DIRECT

I decided to give Jenise a little bit of time to think through some things and to come back around to her customary state of emotional balance. I preferred not to engage with her while she was in that state of irrationality, mainly because my intuition told me to pullback or risk words being exchanged that would have detrimental consequences. I know that miscommunications can occur quite regularly during the retrograde period and so I figured that after the retrograde ended that we would be able to work out our differences. Our misunderstanding occurred with about 10 days left in the retrograde period.

Mercury is in retrograde for about three weeks and then has a shadow period that has an influence, although not as strongly as the actual retrograde period, for an additional couple of weeks. The effects from the shadow period can also be felt for the two-week period prior to going into retrograde.

The day that Mercury went direct fell on a Saturday. I was planning to text her that morning, but she beat me to the punch.

"Thanks for checking on me," her sarcastic text read.

"I knew you were alright. I prayed for you... You feeling better?"

"A little bit. I still want to talk though…"

"Yeah, me too. I feel like the retrograde had us all mixed up, so I decided to let the situation breathe a little bit. I had faith that the universe would sort things out… Come over. Let's talk..." I texted.

"OMW," her text replied within about 20 seconds.

Jenise lived about 15 minutes away from me, but I swear it seemed like she got to my place in seven minutes. About five seconds before she arrived I started Jorja Smith's version of the song "Lost," which turned out to be the perfect song at the perfect time.

"I missed you so much!" she said as she embraced me tightly with both arms. "I'm sorry I left like that. I swear to you, I do not usually act like that. Something came over me," she said as she mixed her tears with laughter.

"Look. I have no desire to be with anyone else. That's first. Please understand this: I like the shit out of you. Do you get that?"

"You like me? After all this time together, all you're willing to admit to is liking me? Really, dude?" she said as she begin to lose her cool again.

"Wait, let me put this a different way... I'm pretty confident that our feelings are mutual. So if you want to talk about that, I'm down to talk about that. I have no problem having this discussion with you. Whatever discussion you want to have... We can have that discussion."

"Dude, you have to do better than that. Really, man?"

"Really, what? What do you want from me that I'm not giving you or willing to give to you? What is it?"

"You know what!" she screamed, reminding me for the third time that morning that the sun was in Sagittarius when she was born.

"I do know the type of conversation that you want to have and I think we should just have it. Obviously you have some things on your mind and in your heart. I know it's not always easy to put those things into words, but I'm willing to give you the time and opportunity to express exactly what it is that you're feeling."

"I don't know what I'm feeling! I was hoping maybe you could tell me how you feel, and I thought that maybe that would help me understand what the hell it is that I'm feeling," she said while trying to calm her cry.

I really wanted to save her from her current state, but something deep down inside insisted that I resist the temptation to come in and save the day.

"Say something! Tell me you love me! Tell me you want to be with me... Tell me something! Just say something, please!" she cried out.

I looked into her eyes and I made sure that all of the love that I had for her was on full display. "Listen," I said gently. "Every time that I look into your eyes I'm trying my best to confess to you how I feel about you. I can't help it. And now that I know that you're ready to hear me vocalize how I'm feeling, here it is... I try my best every single day to be pleasing to the Most High in hopes that I earn His favor that I can then use to keep you in my life... I pray for your safety and your happiness more than I pray for my own... I'm an Aquarius, and I've always valued my freedom... But I feel the most free... I feel the most free when I'm with you... I can be my most divine self when I'm with you... I feel like the man that can save the world when I'm with you and I know that it's not a misunderstanding... You are my secret weapon and I'm aware of it. And if we can just take it one day at a time, I promise that my intention is to spend all my days with you. I see no end in sight."

I felt the ground shaking as she tried to speak but she struggled to speak one clear word. She bent over to try to regroup.

"You still want to talk?" I asked.

"I love you too," she said quickly in between breaths. After about 15 seconds she continued, "I prayed for a man that would pray for me... And not just pray to have me or possess me. But pray for my well-being. Someone who would love me for me and you adore the shit out of me," she said as she started to cry once again.

I was tempted to put my arms around her, but something told me to just stand there and be patient. After about 30 seconds she started to speak once again.

"So you love me, huh?" she said in good spirits.

"Hell yeah. I love the shit out of you, girl," I said as I stepped in a little closer and positioned my face about an inch from hers.

She started to kiss me immediately. I felt a wall come down that I didn't know was there. I thought that we had gotten past any barriers between us, but when she removed that last barrier I felt that she had just at that moment decided to trust that me and our situation would be for her greater good. I was determined to keep it that way, and the alchemist in you can also create the reality that you desire.

Jordan Young

CHAPTER 9
PARADIGM SHIFT

"Jordan," Jenise said softly to get my attention as I stood in the kitchen chopping vegetables.

"Hey, what's up?" I responded only turning my head for a brief second.

She hesitated for a few seconds before continuing, "Do you think the Most High ever tests us?"

"Of course… All the time. Why?"

"Just asking you to speculate, of course, but why do you suppose the Most High chooses to test us?"

This was a tough question, and I had an idea of where the conversation was going. My first thought was to say that He wants to test our faithfulness and see where we are in our development, but I quickly realized that it didn't make much sense if I were to also believe that the Most High sees all and knows all. But, nonetheless, I loved the questions that she grew accustomed to asking me. She always made me think and go within to my most divine and intellectual place. She is definitely partially responsible for much of the wisdom that is available to my conscious mind.

"What do you think?" she asked again.

"Actually, what just hit me is that the Most High wants us to see the results of the test so that we may seek to evolve in the areas that we are weak. My cosmic download is telling me that the tests are for us more so than for the Most High. Wow, I've actually never thought about it like this…"

"When I test you, what do you think is the reason?"

It was at that moment when I first realized the value of female testing, not just for women but for men also. It was certainly a paradigm shift as I now realized that a woman testing me reveals to me the areas in which I am weak and can seek to evolve. With our telepathic relationship, she immediately knew that I had experienced a sudden and dramatic shift of opinion.

"This is the thing… A feminine woman wants a man to lead, protect, and provide. By provide, I'm talking about more than just money and security. I'm talking about stability first and foremost, and emotional stability is at the top of the list. If a man is thrown off by our tests, how can a woman trust that he'll remain a stable leader as he encounters the trials and tribulations of life? And if a woman's tests cause disharmony, that is likely a message from the universe to adjust, adapt, or change. That's at least my opinion," she said.

"How about you test me right now?" I said seductively as I was once again turned on by her intellect and ability to stimulate my mental.

"Test you how?" she asked catching on to my sexual vibe.

I summoned her closer with my index finger, and we made love for two hours before falling asleep together on the kitchen floor. We woke up in the middle of the night and I led her to my room after throwing away the vegetables that were left out. Before going back to sleep, we stared in each other's eyes, smiled, and laughed in bed, but we didn't say a word. I actually preferred it this way. I've always wanted a love that could hear me, feel me, and understand me without verbal communication.

It's still hard to believe that I now see the

value of female testing. When a man passes a test from his woman, he is assured that, at least at that moment, he is strong in that area and has likely been taking good care of his karma as well. A wise woman knows this at least on a subconscious level and that is why she proudly embraces her opportunity to join forces with the universe to promote growth within her man. Also, many of a woman's tests are done unintentionally and without her knowledge. In many cases, she is simply being used by the universe for the greater good.

However, don't get me wrong. If a man and a woman have agreed to be in a committed union, the universe will hold both of them accountable for their actions. If a woman in a committed relationship decides to act sexually inappropriate with another man, this is not a test. Instead, this would be a transgression that the man may have manifested and that the woman will have to deal with karmically at some time in the future.

I now fully understand the idea that every great man has a great woman behind him. Although it may only be his mom, sister, cousin, or friend, the universe certainly uses the women in a man's life to help him to evolve, often one challenge or test at a time.

The problem is that not everyone is open to growth. When faced with an opportunity to evolve, many people, especially those without spiritual literacy, seek to correct the problem by dealing with the person that they believe is responsible instead of going within to heal the person that is truly responsible.

As long as I maintained honest and god-worthy intentions, I could be assured that Jenise's testing of me would be in my best interest as I would not only be able to check on my karma but also my state of strength based on my own internal reactions to the testing. A king has to be stable mentally, physically, spiritually, and emotionally. A female's testing, especially when done by a female with your best interest at heart, helps you to align with your own standards as an exalted male.

If it is not your desire to be an exalted male, a woman's testing is likely to expose such reality to both you and your partner. It is true that many men with bad intentions appear to pass a woman's testing, but he knows within that he failed and, like I said, the testing is for the benefit of the man just as much as it is to the woman. A man with less-than-desirable intentions may be able to not expose his disharmony to a failed test, but he certainly feels the disharmony as it permeates his entire being.

I know there are probably a lot of readers who wonder about the extreme acts of testing for which some women engage. I say that the man should go within and try to figure out how he attracted such a disharmonious situation. The same thing for a man testing a woman or a woman being deeply affected by the actions of a man. I've learned that a man or a woman must always be willing to go within to deal with any amount of disharmony, and by doing so he or she gains access to his or her power as the master of his or her own fate.

The next morning, I arose to Jenise loudly playing "Your Love" by Nicki Minaj. Next she played "Please Me" by Cardi B and Bruno Mars. We didn't usually listen to a lot of rap, with the exception of Nipsey Hussle, because we were aware of its impact to both the conscious and subconscious minds. Although we gave into temptation on occasion and listened to a little gangster rap here and there, we tried to only listen to music with positive vibrations. But back to the story and, besides, who doesn't like a little Cardi B? She was born on the 11th, which makes her naturally inspirational.

Like most lovers, I was usually offered an exclusive glimpse into her mental state based on the music that she chose. "Damn, she wants some more?" I thought to myself as I heard her singing along with the song. I was a little tired still, but I could tell that she was full of energy. I visualized her being in my living room copying Cardi B's dance moves and facial expressions from the video and I was right.

When I walked into the living room, her energy was too sensual and delightful to ignore. I immediately slid behind her to dance with her. Her high energy was contagious. We started bumping and grinding in front of the television that was playing the Cardi B video on YouTube. I knew that she wanted it again and so I gave it to her right there on my living room dance floor. My expressions of love are limitless, and I think she wanted to see for herself. And so I showed her again, again, and again.

CHAPTER 10
AS WITHIN, SO WITHOUT

It was Friday morning and I had a 10:00 AM appointment scheduled with a potential client who was looking to gain some financial stability and prepare for a financially-secure future for her and her three children. Although spirituality is my thing, I love helping people with money matters. I understand how important money is and also how hard it is for a lot of people to focus on consistently doing the right thing when they feel insecure financially.

While I was waiting for my 10:00 AM appointment I was sending positive mental vibes to Jenise from my office chair. I believe in the sayings of "as within, so without" and "as above, so below." I believe that the energy that you release on the mental and spiritual planes has a way of manifesting on the physical plane. Therefore, I made it a consistent habit to think lovely thoughts about Jenise and sweet talk her from afar.

After a long day of sweet talking her from many miles away, I could always tell that she heard me throughout the day based on the way that she looked at me when she saw me again. I realized being with Jenise that foreplay starts in the morning and extends throughout the day. Foreplay is mental and spiritual long before it gets physical. Unfortunately, however, this also means that if I were to send negative vibrations her way that they would likely manifest into an argument or some form of tension on the physical plane. It is my belief that many relationships could be immediately healed if one or both partners started sending positive, loving vibrations to the other on the mental and spiritual planes.

Having knowledge of this fact, I decided to send some positive mental and spiritual vibes to my potential client who was coming in at 10:00 AM. When she arrived, she appeared to have received my vibrations as she was all smiles. I could tell that the Most High put her at ease about our working relationship. At that moment, I realized that she was a client who was divinely sent my way for all that I had to offer, and I was looking forward to being a great benefit to her life. I love adding value to the lives of others. It makes me feel like I deserve to be here on Earth. A part of me believes that if a person isn't consistently loving others by deed, he is wasting a body that could be better used by someone else.

During the meeting, we decided on a 30-year term life insurance policy for around $20 a month. The policy amount was $250,000. We also opened a Roth IRA and put the yearly maximum of $6,000 into the account right away. I put all of her money in the XLK technology sector exchange traded fund, which is a fund that holds many of the largest and most profitable technology companies in the world.

I shared with her that between 2009 and early 2019, XLK had averaged over 18% a year and that was before the then-current 1.6% dividend yield. Like I do with all of my clients, I had her signup for dividend reinvestment, which allows the brokerage firm to use quarterly dividend payments to buy more shares for the client's account without charging any transaction fees. I showed her some sample figures and she was blown away at the long-term increase in wealth just by reinvesting the dividends.

She had been curious about buying individual stocks, but I warned her that even great companies can dramatically drop in value or remain stagnant for years while the general market is rising. I convinced her that there is nothing cool about a person's investments not participating in a bull market, the name when asset prices are consistently increasing. Also, I informed her that focusing on individual stocks, due to their volatile nature, steals a lot of time, energy, and focus away from the person's true purpose. She agreed that her purpose of providing guidance to the youth should not be hindered by the emotional ups and downs of the stock market. I told her that a single stock can go to $0. However, a quality fund, such as XLK, will likely always bounce back after recessions and bear markets, which is the name for when stocks drop by 20% or more from their peak. A correction is when stocks drop by 10% or more. I also was able to convince her to take advantage of future bear markets by investing a little extra when stocks are down by at least 20%.

Before our meeting ended I was able to share with her some of my views on spirituality and she loved and appreciated every word. I'm always happy when I can have an impact on another person, especially when it's appreciated. Her eyes got really big when I disclosed to her that I was vegan. She said that it was something that she had been considering ever since she saw the documentaries *What the Health*, *Earthlings*, and *Forks Over Knives*. She said that she had no idea that the animals were being treated so badly and that eating animals was so bad for our health. She said that she actually grew up thinking that animals were raised peacefully on farms and after dying of natural causes were then sent to the slaughterhouses.

She said that it shocked her to the core when she became aware of the mass killing of animals. She said that she had no idea that humanity could be so cruel and that she cried for days after seeing the documentaries. Since she said that chicken was the last thing that she was holding on to, I showed her some pictures of my fried oyster mushrooms and fried cauliflower wings. She was impressed and said that she'd try them immediately.

After my meeting, I saw that Jenise had called and left a short voicemail. I only had a few minutes before a team meeting and so I called her back without listening to the voicemail.

"Hello," she said in her customary feminine

voice.

"Hey, baby, how are you?"

"I'm good… Are you over there thinking about me again?"

"Why?" I asked with a smile on my face.

"You know why… You got me over here tingling and shit…"

"Sounds like you can't wait until I get home…"

"Actually, I'm not going to wait. I'm about to get on the elevator right now. I'm at your job."

"Wow, are you serious? I have a meeting in like one minute."

"A meeting with a client?"

"Nah, it's a team meeting."

"Oh, well, you're going to have to cancel that because I'm coming up right now. You better think of a lie to tell your team."

I hung up the phone and went into the meeting room. I told the team that Jenise was on her way up and that she needed to see me right away to discuss something that was very important to her. My whole team was in love and so everyone understood.

When Jenise came into my office, the first thing she did was close the blinds. She then locked the door and told Alexa to play "Listen" by 11:11, which is the song I listened to on repeat in the car after meeting her at the bookstore. She then put her finger to her lips as if to tell me to be quiet. I was thinking that she was about to be the loud one and she certainly was. She tried to restrain from making any noise, but I intentionally made it very difficult for her.

Office sex has always been a favorite of mine. I don't think anyone heard us, but, secretly, I enjoy when others hear me satisfying my woman. I'm not sure why, but it feels good. I can only hope that the Most High doesn't mind this tendency of mine because my ultimate goal is to be pleasing to the Most High before anyone else. But I really do love satisfying Jenise in a multitude of ways. She's my gift; that I know for sure. No woman this special could ever be anything less. Looking at her reminded me of how great I was at my best, and she was always pushing me to go deeper and deeper, spiritually, mentally, and sexually. I knew that I was developing into what most would consider a superhero and she was my co-star.

When I got home the party continued until the middle of the night. We rarely ever made love for just an hour or two like most normal healthy couples. She had a key to my apartment and had been spending most of her time at my place. When I got home she was waiting on the arm of my sofa with just a button down shirt on and it was open.

"Guess what?" she said seductively.

"What?" I asked as we locked eyes.

"I was thinking about you this time..."

"Oh, yeah?"

"Yep," she said and then signaled for me to come closer with her index finger. She then said, "Alexa, play my Alina Baraz playlist.

The first song that came on was "Make You Feel" by Alina Baraz and Galimatias. The next song was "Show Me" by the same duo. It then switched over to Sabrina Claudio's "Belong to You" and "Stand Still." The last song that I remember from her playlist before we both left Earth and visited the cosmos was "Rodeo" by Jacquees and T-Pain. From the first time that she played music for me I knew that we were going to go the distance. It's something intoxicating about getting in sync musically with your lover, and music has helped to facilitate some of our most exciting times together.

CHAPTER 11
IN PERPETUITY

The next morning we did a 30-minute yoga video together. In addition to being a great exercise, yoga has a way of helping you to align with your true self and true purpose. I put it in the same family as meditation, prayer, sun gazing, and walking outside with your bare feet in the dirt. The video that we did was pretty intense and we stayed on the floor for about 10 minutes after the video ended.

"Last night was good," she said with a smile.

"You mean when you tried to chock me to death with my tie?" I said referring to when she got on top when "Rodeo" came on and she held on by my neck tie as she acted out her cowgirl fantasies.

"You're weren't going to die…"

"What would you do if I did?"

"Tell the Most High to take me too."

"What if I already have a woman when you get to heaven?"

"I'd probably kill her," she said nonchalantly.

"Oh, my god. You can't just go around killing angels. What's wrong with you?"

"She know you belong to me. I wish one of them heffas would step to you. I swear to god I would kill her."

"Oh, my god. Dude, you can't say that. That's probably how you got kicked out of heaven last time."

"So... Don't mess with my man. If any angels in heaven got they eye on you they better listen up to what I'm saying... They don't want these problems... I'd do it in front of the Most High too. They've officially been warned cause I know they can hear me."

"Wait, are you serious right now?"

"You think I'm not, babe? As above, so below, remember? You mines down here and up there. Don't get one of them girls hurt up there. And then I might smack you too when I'm done with her because you should've known I was coming."

She knew how to make me feel really good about choosing her as my partner in crime. I was invested in her and she was invested in me. I was hoping to make her my partner for life and she was thinking about eternity. I was with it all the way.

"You can't be coming to heaven with a bad attitude. You might get us both kicked out cause if you have to leave I'm leaving too. We're a package deal in heaven or hell," I replied.

"You'd really go to hell with me, baby?"

"Not ideally, so don't be getting us in trouble. And plus the devil is probably a hater and likely wouldn't even let us be together. So I'd be in hell for nothing with a bunch of women I don't have any interest in."

"So... you'd really go to hell with me?"

"I already did once before. You don't remember? Second time couldn't be too much worse."

"Jordan, what are you talking about, babe?"

I immediately realized that I had my foot in my mouth. I didn't want to tell her how hard those two months were for me after our first night together, but I knew that she wasn't about to just let it go. Something just told me to be honest and so I confessed.

"Those two months that you were away... That was really hard for me. You have no idea what ya boy went through. I mean, I was strong and all, but it wasn't easy."

"Did you cry?"

"Hell naw!" I said as we both started laughing. "Not on the outside at least. I might have cried on the inside a little bit," I said with a smile.

"You wanted me?"

"I let you come back, didn't I?"

"True… What would you do if I left again?"

"Every day I'd take selfies with random women and send them to you with the hashtag single life."

"I wish you would. You better not play with me."

"Well if you leave, that's what you have to look forward to."

"I'd find and kill every girl in your pictures. I think you should stop playing with me," she said seriously but sweetly.

"You would really kill for me?"

"And you too! I'd kill you too. I'm serious, nigga," she said using the n-word for the first time ever in front of me.

We started playfully wrestling on the floor. I was gentle, but I used just enough strength to have my way. When I got on top of her I held her arms down.

"Who you gonna kill now? I should tickle you for talking all that trash," I said.

"Please don't tickle me!" she screamed nervously.

"I don't like when people threaten me..."

"I'm sorry. I swear I'm sorry. Please don't tickle me. Please, please, please."

"What you gonna give me if I don't?"

"I'll do whatever you say. I promise."

"Anything?"

"Yes! Anything. Just please don't tickle me," she said while laughing.

"I want you to spell my name in alphabetical order. And you have 10 seconds."

"What! Oh, my god. Okay, wait. J-A. I messed up! Wait! A-D-J-N-O-R!" she said quickly.

"Look at you. You're good under pressure, huh?"

"Didn't you know? I'm good at everything..."

"You're so cocky."

"You seem to like it..."

"Only cause I'm scared you're going to kill somebody if I don't."

"Whatever... As long as we have an understanding, I'm good with whatever."

"This is not an understanding," I said causing us both to laugh.

That Saturday afternoon we went to the Dallas farmers market and tried all of the vegan food that we could find. My favorite was the oyster mushrooms, but one of the places had some really good vegan tacos. We both ate way too much food, so we spent two hours in the gym Saturday evening. When we got back to my place after leaving the gym we decided to watch something on YouTube.

"What do you want to watch?" she asked.

"In the mood for Dr. Sebi?"

"Not tonight… What else you got?"

"Let's listen to *The Science of Getting Rich* by Wallace D. Wattles. It's one of my favorite money books of all time."

"Jordan, I love that book! I haven't read it in a long time though. Yeah, let's listen to that," she said with a ton of excitement.

The audiobook on YouTube was a little over two hours long. After the book ended she was in the mood for a spiritual conversation.

"Do you think we really get to go to heaven or hell when we die?" she asked.

"That's a good question, but I'm not sure if there's a way to ever even know. I guess we can only speculate."

"So speculate."

"My first thought is that heaven is the domain of the Most High, but I think if we live in alignment with the Most High to the best of our ability that we can experience heaven right here on Earth. I agree that the kingdom of heaven is within us if only we know ourselves, align with our true selves, and seek to be pleasing to the Most High. I think the bliss that we feel when we're together is comparable to what a person would expect of heaven… But I think we should definitely live mindful of the fact that we may have to stand face-to-face with the Highest Power and answer for our intentions and deeds after we die… What do you think?"

"Is that how you got me? By sucking up to the Most High?"

"Hey, if it works it works," I said with a smile.

"I like what you said. I agree that there is no way for us to know for sure. I think heaven and hell is what you make it… I think the energy that we put into the universe determines if we are to be in heaven or hell at any given moment… I agree with you that perfect harmony is like heaven. I know that with you I am all the way happy, and I wouldn't trade this feeling for anything in the world. Even if I could sit at the right hand of the Most High… If you can't come with me, it wouldn't be heaven for me… This is my heaven right here," she said with an abundance of sincerity as she leaned in to kiss me on the sofa.

I really enjoyed kissing Jenise. Not just this time but every time. It was always an experience even when it didn't lead to sex. I can only imagine that she enjoyed kissing me as well because every time we made love throughout the night we would lock lips for at least an hour non-stop. So much passion. So much love. So much inspiration. So much excitement. As crazy as it sounds, it actually made me very happy to hear Jenise threaten all of the women in heaven. One thing was certain without a doubt: she was created for me and I was created for her.

CHAPTER 12
THE AGE OF AQUARIUS

Being vegan was very important to me. When I first discovered how animals were treated I was sick to my stomach, and I knew that I had to do something. I was compelled to act on their behalf just like Tupac Shakur, Malcom X, Nelson Mandela, and Muhammad Ali were compelled to speak for the voiceless during their times. As an African-American, or highly melanated, man in America, I too cared about the problems faced by our community. However, after gaining knowledge of self and of the universe, I knew that it was a better use of energy to go within to heal and create harmony as opposed to trying to change external forces. Remember, as within, so without and as above, so below.

I knew that it was silly for Black people to participate in the unnecessary torture and killing of innocent animals, despite their loud cries and screams for mercy, and then expect for our prayers to be heard when we ask for freedom and justice that knows no boundaries. Once you understand that the universe has laws, it is easy to then innerstand how harmony is created, restored, and destroyed.

As a compassionate, forgiving, and loving people, I knew that we, as melanated people, had a responsibility to contribute our gifts to the world. The best way to contribute your gift is to lead by example, so I knew that us as melanated people couldn't continue to participate in such barbaric atrocities and then complain about someone being unfair to us. It actually shows, to some degree, how much our people have been conditioned, poisoned, and intentionally led astray.

Since going vegan I had built a reputation as a powerful spiritual and financial teacher and speaker. I decided to write a letter to every large Black organization all over the country that I thought was truly concerned with the spiritual and financial development of our people. I explained to them how universal law can be used by all to restore harmony for all and also how it can be used by a particular individual to create harmony for that individual. I also wrote about the importance of loving and respecting all living things.

I stood fast on the position that, based on my innerstanding of universal law, the melanated community has somehow manifested its current state of reality. However, I also guaranteed that the Most High would bring peace to everyone who stopped contributing to animal suffering and who also tried their best to live in alignment with universal law. It was just that simple if we were to experience true freedom and justice that knows no boundaries. No need to march. No need to kick, scream, or shout. Just look to the Most High, instead of our oppressors, and align. That's it...

Somehow, one of my letters reached a prominent African-American member of Congress who, along with the Speaker of the House, invited me to speak to the full body of Congress. He emailed me and stated that his spirit had compelled him to reach out to me and that a strong feeling had come over his body that time was of the essence concerning this issue. He too was vegan, but he said that he had never realized how our disregard and participation in animal suffering had contributed to our own state of degradation.

He knew that if we could get the word out that the world would immediately change for the better, at least for all that participated in aligning to the best of their ability with universal law. He said that he understood the logic in saying that if you intentionally cause suffering, you too shall be made to suffer.

I now had a very powerful ally on the physical plane. I already knew that the Most High was my most faithful ally overall as it was His work that I was attempting to execute. Remember, as a child, it was the Most High who I talked to and promised to do whatever work that He needed from me. I was now in a position to possibly save billions of human and animal lives if my work was a success. I was also in position to help make world peace a reality. I knew that once we have respect for animals that our respect and consideration would evolve to include all other humans, plants, trees, and the oceans. Humanity would then transcend the pains of the lower plane and vibrate on the higher for as long as we worked diligently to honor the Most High and remain in alignment with universal law.

As far as Jenise is concerned, she was my biggest supporter and she was with me every step of the way. Remember, she was my secret weapon, and I prayed often that I would never forget that. Many of my blessings were stored within her and she lovingly delivered them to me. Before my speech on Capitol Hill, she presented me with a beautiful gold ankh necklace. She said that she wanted me to have every resource that was available to me and she knew that I would vibrate the city of Washington, D.C. with my speech, and I did my best to make her words a reality.

After delivering my speech on Capitol Hill, even the most conservative lawmakers were either in tears or clearly sympathetic to every word that I spoke. I didn't realize it until my speech was over, but I was drowning in sweat. I knew that the Most High was on my side using me as a vessel because I had never spoken such powerful words as eloquently as I did that day in Washington. My speech on Capitol Hill garnered worldwide attention and I received an immediate invite to speak to the United Nations.

Three weeks after my speech on Capitol Hill, I was in New York delivering my message to the United Nations, and I was received with the same love, respect, and compassion as I had in Washington, D.C. After leaving New York, I received assurances from both members of the U.S. Congress and member nations of the United Nations that they would immediately bring forth legislation to outlaw animal cruelty, which included murdering healthy, innocent animals for food or any other animal byproduct. I was promised that they would seek to immediately close all slaughterhouses and that the issue would be treated as a national emergency. Although I knew that the work wasn't over, I knew that in time my work would have contributed to the saving of billions of human and animal lives. Our planet would be saved and world peace would soon follow.

I decided to marry Jenise in a non-traditional ceremony. Jenise and I didn't like the idea of adding the government to our relationship, which is what traditional marriage does. We both thought that a marriage should be between man, woman, and the Most High, not between man, woman, the Most High, and the state. We invited about 200 friends and family members, who were all impressed with the variety and tastiness of our vegan food options.

We traveled the world together after our union, which allowed me to speak to college and high school students all over the globe and deliver my message to those who, in the future, would be responsible for safekeeping our planet. I was happy, she was happy, and the Most High had shown Himself to be All Supreme. Welcome, you are now in the Age of Aquarius...

ABOUT THE AUTHOR

Jordan Young is the pen name for an African-American author, investor, and avid vegan. He lives in Texas and loves investing, teaching, and having spiritual conversations. For movie rights or other business, contact veganlovejones@gmail.com.

Lightning Source UK Ltd.
Milton Keynes UK
UKHW020949050123
414865UK00011B/1516